Bill Bevan

Simon's Magic Bobble Hat

Illustrated by Sally Holmes

PUFFIN BOOKS

PUFFIN BOOKS

Published by the Penguin Group
27 Wrights Lane, London W8 5TZ, England
Viking Penguin Inc., 40 West 23rd Street, New York, New York 10010, USA
Penguin Books Australia Ltd, Ringwood, Victoria, Australia
Penguin Books Canada Ltd, 2801 John Street, Markham, Ontario, Canada L3R 1B4
Penguin Books (NZ) Ltd, 182–190 Wairau Road, Auckland 10, New Zealand

Penguin Books Ltd, Registered Offices: Harmondsworth, Middlesex, England

First published by Viking Kestrel 1988
Published in Puffin Books 1989
10 9 8 7 6 5 4 3 2 1

Printed and bound in Great Britain by
Cox & Wyman Ltd, Reading

Contents

Simon and the Supermarket Trolley

It was Saturday morning. Mum was going to the supermarket.

"Can we come too?" asked Simon and his sister, Fiona.

"All right," said Mum.

"I want to push the trolley," said Simon.

"OK – but only if you're very
careful," replied Mum.

When they got to the
supermarket, Mum pulled out a
trolley from the line by the entrance.

"There you are," she said.
"Don't bump into anyone."

Simon pushed the trolley
between the rows of shelves

while Fiona and Mum put the
shopping in it.

Soon the trolley was nearly
full. Simon pretended it was a
truck and that the shelves were
houses on each side of a street.
He had to steer the truck down
the street and around the other
shoppers.

Simon was good at steering, but one of the front wheels of the trolley was making a squeaking noise. Sometimes it twiddled round and round, making the trolley swing from side to side.

First the trolley swerved to the right.

Then it swerved to the left.

It ought to have a horn, thought Simon.

Then suddenly it turned and bumped into a big pile of tins of baked beans, which were built up like a sort of castle, taller than Simon.

The tins tumbled down with a

great clatter and rolled across
the floor. Simon jumped back
and before he knew what had
happened he had bumped into a
shelf full of bottles of tomato
sauce! The bottles smashed on

the floor. Tomato sauce began to ooze out everywhere. There was an awful mess.

"Now look what you've done!" cried Mum. "You weren't looking where you were going!"

It isn't fair, thought Simon. It wasn't *his* fault that the trolley wouldn't go where he pointed it. Stupid trolley!

A man in a white coat rushed up, followed by an assistant carrying a mop and bucket.

"I'm terribly sorry," said Mum. "It *was* an accident!"

The man in the white coat began to pick up the tins while the assistant mopped up the tomato sauce.

Mum took the trolley away from Simon and gave it to Fiona, and she pushed it to the check-out point.

"You are clumsy, Simon," Fiona said. "No wonder Mummy was angry."

Fiona was two years older than Simon. She never seemed

15

to get into trouble like Simon did.

After Mum had paid for the shopping, she told Fiona she could push the trolley to the car.

"Can't I push it?" said Simon.

16

"You might bump into one of
the cars," said Mum. "We've
had enough trouble for one
day."

Squeak, squeak, squeak went
the trolley as Fiona pushed it
across the car-park. Squeak,
squeak . . . *crash*!

The trolley toppled over on its side. All the shopping spilled out!

"Oh, Mummy," said Fiona. "Look – the front wheel's come right off!"

Mum looked at the broken wheel. "No wonder the trolley was wobbling about," she said. "It wasn't Simon's fault at all!"

"Told you so!" said Simon, under his breath.

Then he helped Fiona pick up the shopping and carry it to the car.

When they got home, they all unloaded the car.

"Next time we go shopping,

Simon," Mum said, "we'll look for a trolley that doesn't have wonky wheels. Then you can push it all through the supermarket and all the way back to the car!"

Simon's Yellow Bike

"**H**urry up and finish your breakfast, children," said Mum one morning. "Grandad has invited us down to his farm for the day."

"Can we feed the ducks and chickens?" Fiona asked.

"I expect so," said Mum.

"Stupid chickens," said Simon. "Why can't we go to the zoo?"

"Because your Grandad has

a present for you. Something
that he promised you a long
time ago. It's a surprise."

"Oh!" said Simon.

He gobbled up his cornflakes
and finished his milk. Then he
rushed to get the warm coat,
green wellies and woolly hat

that he always wore on the farm.

How exciting! he thought. He couldn't imagine what Grandad's present could be.

Grandad had hidden Simon's surprise present. Simon looked everywhere for it, and at last he found it in the barn. It was just

what he had always wanted – a two-wheeler bike!

It was just the right size for him to ride and had lights that worked and a horn.

Simon was very excited. He rode the bike round and round the farmyard. Then Grandad asked if Fiona and Simon would like to see the new litter of piglets.

"Oh yes!" said Fiona.

Simon followed Grandad and Fiona on his yellow bike.

There were ten little piglets, just three weeks old. They were scampering around, rolling in the mud and playing like a lot of fat puppies, while the mother pig looked on from the next pen. Grandad leant over and scratched her back with the tip of his stick.

Next they fed the ducks and the chickens and two big white geese, and then Grandad led the way to a field where cows were grazing.

Suddenly, in a field next to the cows, Fiona saw a little white pony. It looked just like the circus pony in her picture book.

In the book, the pony was being ridden by a girl who was wearing a beautiful silver dress,

with a sparkling diamond crown
on her head. She looked just
like a fairy princess.

"Oh," sighed Fiona, "I wish I
could ride a pony like that. Is it
a circus pony, Grandad?"

"Why, yes," said Grandad.
"She's called Snowflake. She's
too old for the circus now, so

I've given her a home on the farm."

Grandad went into the barn and came out with a rope which he called a halter. He put it around Snowflake's neck. Then he lifted Fiona up on to the pony's back.

"Hold on to her mane," said

Grandad. Fiona held on tightly
to the stiff, bristly hair.

Grandad clicked his tongue
and Snowflake began to walk
slowly round the field with
Grandad walking beside her,
holding the halter.

30

Fiona clung more tightly to the pony's mane and pretended she was the girl in the beautiful silver dress, and that she could hear the circus band and people clapping and cheering her.

Simon soon got tired of watching Fiona, so he rode his bike back to the farmyard and went to see the piglets again.

He thought they might like to have their backs scratched. He looked around for a stick, but the only one he could see was pushed down through a loop of wire on the gate to the piglets' pen.

Simon pulled the stick out. He couldn't reach the piglets with it, so he opened the gate . . .

Oh dear! First one piglet wriggled between Simon's legs and escaped. Then another . . . and another . . . and another!

Soon there were ten little piglets, all squeaking with excitement, running around the

farmyard, snuffling and rooting
about in every corner, chasing
the chickens, dodging the
ducks, teasing the geese.

What a scene it was! The
chickens were clucking, the

34

ducks were quacking, the geese were honking and the mother pig, who couldn't get out of her pen, was making a terrible fuss.

The noise was so loud that Grandad and Jack, the man who looked after Grandad's cows, came running to find out what was going on.

Jack and Grandad set about catching the piglets.

Simon tried his best to help, but the piglets were too quick and slippery for him.

Then he had a good idea. He
rode his yellow bike after the
piglets and beeped on his horn
to turn them back towards
Grandad and Jack.

At last all the little piglets
had been caught and were
safely back in their pen.

"I'm sorry I opened the gate, Grandad," said Simon.

His Grandad laughed. "No harm done – but it's the first time I've seen a herd of piglets being rounded up by a yellow bike! Why ever didn't we think of that before?"

Simon's Magic Bobble Hat

"We're going on holiday," Mum said one morning.

"Oh great," said Fiona. "Can we play on the beach and go in the sea?"

"Not this time," said Mum. "There are mountains and lakes where we're going, and there's lots of snow. You can make snowballs and snowmen – and Simon can wear his bobble hat."

38

She got the hat from the cupboard. It was bright blue, with yellow stripes and a yellow, woolly bobble on the top.

Mum pulled the hat over Simon's head.

'You *do* look smart," she said. "You won't get lost in a crowd when you're wearing a hat like that!"

On the way to the airport, Simon was disappointed when he wasn't allowed to sit in the front of the taxi with the driver. But when they arrived, Mum let him help push the baggage trolley.

She said they might have to wait a long time to have their tickets checked, so Simon and Fiona could have a look round the airport shop.

"And put on your bobble hat," she told Simon, "or you'll lose it."

The shop sold magazines,

sweets and lots of toys. Simon
liked the space stations and the
robots and the creepy-looking
giants' castles and the monster-
stomping trucks.

But Fiona was bored. "Oh,
do come *on*!" she said. "Mummy
said we could buy some
sweets."

Simon shook his head.

"All right," said Fiona. "The sweets are over there. Don't move – I'll be back in a minute."

But after she had gone, Simon decided he wanted to watch the aeroplanes landing and taking off like they did on television.

He was sure there must be a
window he could see them from.
Fiona wasn't interested in
aeroplanes, anyway. He would
go and explore on his own.

There were lots of people in
the airport. Simon rushed about
anxiously, getting hot and
sticky. He pulled off his hat and
stuffed it in his pocket.

He soon began to feel tired. He couldn't see any window and all he wanted now was to go back to Mum. But where was she?

Simon sat down on a seat to rest. He was lost, and lonely. He started to cry. He sniffed and put his hand in his pocket for a handkerchief. Instead, he pulled out his bobble hat.

Suddenly he remembered what his Mum had said about the hat.

"You won't get lost in a crowd when you're wearing a hat like that!" she had said.

What had she meant? Could

there be some sort of *magic* about the bobble hat?

Simon put the hat on – and when he looked up, there was a lady in uniform standing in front of him.

"Is your name Simon?" she asked him.

She looked a bit like the
lollipop lady at Fiona's school,
so he thought it was probably
all right to talk to her.

"Yes," said Simon. "I'm
going in a plane with my Mum,
but I don't know where she is."

"She's been looking
everywhere for you," said the
lady. "You're lucky I happened

to see your bobble hat. Your
sister said that you were
wearing it when she last saw
you in the shop."

Mum was so pleased to see
Simon that she couldn't be
really angry with him. She
hugged him and gave him a

kiss. Then they hurried to the
plane.

It was exciting when the
jumbo jet raced down the
runway and soared into the air.
Simon pulled his bobble hat
down over his ears and
pretended it was a space
helmet.

And then the magic

happened again! A lady in a
uniform – a different one, this
time – was coming down the
cabin towards him. She stopped
beside his seat.

"Hallo, Simon," she said.
"The Captain heard about you
getting lost at the airport.

Would you like to come into the
cockpit and see how he flies the
plane?"

"Oh, wow!" said Simon.
"Can I?" he asked Mum.

"Of course you can." She
smiled. "But don't get lost this
time, will you?"

Simon pulled his hat down tightly over his ears.

"Not while I'm wearing my magic bobble hat," he said proudly.

Simon and the Baby Duckling

Mum was washing up after lunch.

"It's a lovely day," she said. "Shall we go to the park? We can be home before Fiona comes back from her party."

"Oh, yes!" said Simon. "Can I fly my kite?"

"I don't think there's enough wind," said Mum. "But take

your boat and you can sail it on the lake."

Simon's boat had red sails. When he took it to the lake, Mum tied a long string to it so he could let it sail a long way out from the shore.

When they got to the lake

two other children were sailing their boats. They all had a race and Simon's boat won. Mum fed the ducks with bread. The ducks lived on the lake and had nests on an island in the middle of it.

The ducks gobbled up all the bread. Then they stood on their heads in the water to find any crumbs that had sunk to the bottom.

They looked so funny, wriggling their tails in the air. They made Simon laugh.

When Simon got tired of sailing his boat, Mum gave him the last of their bread so he

could feed the mother duck who
had six little ducklings
swimming after her.

The mother duck swam up
close to Simon and took some of
the bread right out of his hand.

"Can I have an ice-cream?" asked Simon, when they'd finished feeding the ducks.

"All right," said Mum.

They started walking along the path by the lake – and the mother duck began to follow them, with the six little ducklings waddling along behind her.

"Don't take any notice," said Simon's Mum. "They'll soon go back into the water."

But just then a big black dog came bounding along the path, barking at the ducks on the lake.

The frightened ducks flew off

to the island, but the mother
duck stayed where she was,
because her babies were right in
the path of the big black dog.

She hissed at the dog.

The dog growled and this

time the mother duck scuttled
quickly into the water, her little
ducklings following. But one
little duckling was missing. It
was hiding in a big drainpipe in
the wall by the path.

"Oh, the poor wee mite!"
cried a lady who had stopped to
see what was happening. "That
dog shouldn't be running loose
like that. It should be on a
lead!"

They could hear the little
duckling cheeping somewhere

inside the dark drainpipe. The
mother duck and her other five
ducklings were swimming away
to the island.

"We must get the little thing
out," the lady said. "If he
doesn't find his mother quickly,
a cat or a magpie could catch
him. Or a rat."

Mum crouched down and
looked into the pipe.

"It's too dark," she said. "I
can't see anything."

Somewhere at the back of the
pipe the frightened duckling
was still cheeping, calling for its
mother.

Mum put her arm right into
the pipe. "He's too far in," she
said. "I can't reach him."

"There's nothing for it,"
sighed the lady. "We'll just
have to leave him there."

Simon knelt down and looked
into the drainpipe. It was just
big enough for him to squeeze
his head and shoulders inside.

But it was dark and scary in there. The thought of spiders and beetles and earwigs and other creepy-crawlies – even a rat? – made Simon shiver.

But if he *could* crawl in, he might be able to reach the poor little duckling.

Simon lay flat on his tummy and wriggled into the pipe. A cobweb brushed across his face. He stretched out both arms in front of him, but he couldn't reach the duckling.

He wriggled in a bit further . . . and suddenly his hands touched a warm, feathery little bundle. He closed his hands

around the duckling, being careful not to hold it too tightly, and began to wriggle backwards out of the pipe. Mum helped by pulling on his ankles.

At last Simon was able to stand up. He held out his hands and opened them just enough to let Mum see the duckling. It was nibbling at Simon's finger with its soft, flat beak.

"Oh, isn't he a love," said the lady. "But I wouldn't have gone into that hole, my dear, if you had paid me a King's ransom!"

They put the duckling into

the water at the edge of the lake
and it began to swim, calling
anxiously for its mother.

Out on the island the mother
duck heard the little duckling
calling her and began to swim
towards the shore, with the

other five ducklings following her.
   The little duckling swam
eagerly towards them and
reached them at last. Simon
and his Mum watched as they
all turned round and headed
back to the safety of the island.

Simon and the Naughty Puppy

Fiona and Simon had been helping Mum bake some cakes. There were chocolate cakes and currant cakes and treacle tarts and gingerbread men and two great big strawberry flans.

"Can I have some strawberry flan for tea?" Simon asked Mum. He loved strawberries.

"We're not going to *eat* all

those cakes, silly!" said Fiona.
"Mummy's going to sell them at
the school fête tomorrow. She's
going to give the money to a
lady who looks after puppies
and kittens whose owners don't
want them any more.
Everybody calls her the Pets
Lady."

Mum nodded. "We'll see her
at the fête. She's asked me to

find a home for a little puppy
that she's been looking after."

Simon was excited. "Oh,
great! Can we bring him home
with us, Mummy?"

"Well, we'll see," said Mum.

Now when Mum said "We'll
see", sometimes she meant

"Yes" and sometimes she
meant "No".

Simon could hardly wait to
find out what Mum meant this
time.

When they got to Fiona's
school the next day, there were
lots of tables set up on the

playing fields and people were
selling all sorts of things – jams
and pickles, cakes and sweets,
and apples that were polished
till they shone, and clothes,
books and toys that weren't
needed any longer.

There was a children's

roundabout, too, and a Punch and Judy show, and even an ice-cream van, but Simon couldn't think of anything else but the puppy.

"Hurry up, Mummy," he said. "The Pets Lady might give him away to someone else!"

So they left Fiona to spread a clean white cloth on the table and to lay out the cakes on it. She loved playing at shops, and

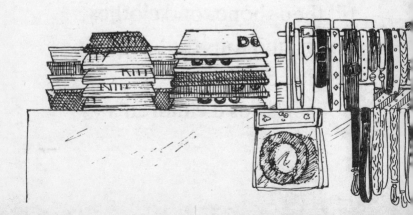

now she would be able to help
sell real cakes.

The Pets Lady was sitting
behind a table piled with dog
collars, leads, rubber balls and
bones that went "click" when a
dog bit them. There were tins of

pet food and all sorts of other things that dogs and puppies and cats and kittens might need.

Sitting beside the table was the cuddliest, roly-poly little puppy that Simon had ever seen.

"Isn't he lovely, Mummy?" said Simon. "Can we have him? Please?"

"Well . . . we'll see," said Mum.

But she smiled, and this time Simon knew that "We'll see" meant "Yes".

The Pets Lady picked up the puppy and put him in Simon's

arms. The puppy wriggled and
wriggled and tried to lick
Simon's nose.

"There," said the Pets Lady,
"he likes you. He's called
Rascal."

The Pets Lady gave Simon a
new red collar and a lead for
Rascal, and Simon proudly led

84

the puppy back towards their table.

At first Rascal was very well-behaved. But a little further along, Mrs Smudge, the school cleaning-lady, was selling home-made lemonade, mint humbugs, fudge and toffee apples – and under the table was her big ginger cat, Miaou, lapping up a saucer of milk.

Miaou didn't like dogs. When she saw Rascal, her fur stood up on end and her tail fluffed out like a bristly bottle-brush.

And then a lot of things began to happen at once.

Miaou spat at Rascal.

Rascal wasn't standing for that, even from a fierce ginger

cat that was almost as big as he was! He pulled his lead out of Simon's hand and dived under the table after Miaou. The end of the lead got tangled around the table leg.

Miaou ran off. Rascal tried to run after her – and the table began to topple over.

The lemonade jug tipped up and *splosh!* went the lemonade all over Rascal. The plates of fudge and mint humbugs slid off the table and the toffee apples rolled over the grass.

Suddenly Rascal's lead pulled free from the table leg. Rascal went chasing off after Miaou, and Mum and Simon went after him, calling, "Stop, Rascal! Stop!"

What a disaster! Simon felt like crying.

What would Mum say?
Would she think Rascal was too
naughty, and give him back to
the Pets Lady? It was all that
ginger cat's fault, nasty, bad-
tempered old thing!

Rascal ran as fast as his little
legs would carry him, but he
was only a puppy and he

couldn't catch up with Miaou. After a while he got tired, and stopped for a rest.

Mum was out of breath when she and Simon finally caught up with Rascal.

"What a naughty dog you are," she scolded. "No wonder they call you Rascal! Now I'll

have to pay poor Mrs Smudge
for everything you've spoiled!''

She felt in her bag for her
purse, but it wasn't there!

"It must have fallen out while
I was chasing Rascal," she said
sadly. "I'll never find it."

But Simon had an idea.

He remembered a clever tracker dog that he had seen on television.

"Rascal could sniff out the purse, Mummy," he said.

Mum didn't really think that Rascal could find her purse, but she let him sniff her bag so that he would know what the purse smelt like. Then Simon led Rascal back the way that he had come.

Rascal trotted along with his nose to the ground.

Then he suddenly dived under a table that was piled high with cups and plates and saucers.

What a CRASH there'd be if Rascal tipped *that* table over!

Simon tugged at the lead and after a moment Rascal came out, wagging his tail and looking pleased with himself. In his mouth he was carrying Mum's purse!

Mum was so pleased she gave Rascal a big hug. Rascal was still a bit wet and sticky from the lemonade, but Mum didn't mind that.

"What a *clever* dog you are," she said.

"Rascal's just like a *real* tracker dog," Simon said, proudly, "and he's going to be my very best friend!"